DISNEY

MINNIE MOUSE

Minnie Mysteries—The Flower Thief
By Catherine Hapka
Illustrated by DiCicco Digital Arts

PaRragon

Bath • New York • Singapore • Hong Kong • Cologne • Delhi
Melbourne • Amsterdam • Johannesburg • Auckland • Shenzhen

One spring day Daisy Duck rang Minnie Mouse's doorbell.
"Hi, Minnie," Daisy said. "I've brought you some marigolds from my garden."

"Daisy, you're a dear!" said Minnie. "They'll look perfect with my daffodils."

"Definitely," Daisy agreed. "Daffodils are my favorite flower."

"Mine too," said Minnie.

But when the friends went out to Minnie's backyard, they had a big surprise.

"My daffodils!" Minnie shrieked. "They're gone!"

"What's happened?" Minnie cried. "They were here yesterday!"

"The stems are still here," Daisy pointed out.

Minnie looked more closely. "You're right," she said. "But the flowers are missing. It looks like someone chopped them off with something sharp."

"This is terrible," Daisy said. "It must be a flower thief!"

"What's this?" Daisy asked a moment later. She pulled a few strands of fuzzy white hair off a bush near the daffodil patch.

"Is it a clue?" Minnie asked. "Maybe the flower thief left it."

"Maybe," Daisy said. "Or maybe it's from Fluffy's bow."

A moment later Minnie's doorbell rang. Mickey Mouse was standing on the porch. "Hi, Minnie," he said shyly. "I've brought you a present." He held out a big bunch of daffodils! And they were tied with a fluffy white ribbon!

"Oh, Mickey," Minnie cried. "How could you? You cut down my daffodils!"

"What do you mean, Minnie?" Mickey exclaimed. "I bought these at Power's Flower Shop because I know daffodils are your favorite flowers!"

Minnie smiled. "Really?" she said. She was glad that Mickey wasn't the flower thief.

Minnie, Daisy, and Mickey decided to look around town for the flower thief. They headed to the park and found Goofy—with a daffodil in his lapel! And he was playing with a yo-yo that had a fuzzy white string!

"Gawrsh, Minnie," Goofy said. "I didn't do it. This daffodil came from Power's Flower Shop. Mr. Power is having a sale on daffodils today."

"Really?" Minnie said. "That's quite a coincidence."

Daisy nodded. "Maybe we'd better check out Mr. Power's flowers. Right now!"

The four friends went to Power's Flowers. They peeked in the window. "That's Mr. Power," Mickey said.

Minnie saw that the shopkeeper had a sharp pair of scissors and a fuzzy white mustache. And his shop was full of daffodils!

"He did it!" she cried. "I know it!"

Minnie and her friends burst into the shop. "Where did you get these daffodils?" Minnie asked.

"From a farmer named Mrs. Pote," Mr. Power answered. "She delivers daffodils here every day. But today she brought dozens of extras!"

Minnie wondered if Mrs. Pote could be the prowler. "Where can we find her?" she continued.

Mr. Power pointed. "That-a-way," he said. "You can't miss her. She has fuzzy white hair."

Mrs. Pote's farm was called Pote's Goats.

"Yes, I delivered extra daffodils today," Mrs. Pote told Minnie. "My favorite goat, Flower, usually eats a lot of them as soon as they bloom. But today she didn't seem very hungry."

That gave Minnie an idea. "May I see Flower?" she asked.
Mrs. Pote led the friends to a pen. But there was no goat inside!

"Oh, dear!" Mrs. Pote cried. "She must have escaped!"

"Look! There's a hole in the fence," Mickey said, pointing.

"Now what do we do?" Daisy exclaimed. "Not only are Minnie's daffodils gone, but so is Mrs. Pote's goat!"

"Hmmm," said Minnie, deep in thought. "Maybe these two mysteries are connected!"

"What do you mean, Minnie?" Daisy asked.

"I just figured out who the flower prowler might be," Minnie explained. "It's someone who really likes daffodils. Someone who likes them even more than we do!"

Daisy held up the fuzzy strands of hair. "Don't forget this," she reminded Minnie. "Isn't it still a clue?"

"It sure is," Minnie agreed. "And so is this!" She pointed toward a trail of footprints. "Just follow me!"

Minnie and the others followed the footprints straight to Daisy's yard. There was Flower, happily munching away.

"See?" Minnie said. "I knew it! There's our flower thief. Now, if we could only train her to like weeds instead!"

The End